27 Years of Life

Collection of Poems

ASHAKI SATOMI SCOTT

27 Years of Life
Collection of Poens

ISBN: 979-8-218-66655-2

Published in the United States

Dedication

This book is dedicated to anyone who has felt like at one point in their life, their voice was taken from them. For those who couldn't speak their truth or maybe didn't know how to even articulate it and put it into words. It's for everyone who is on their self love journey, healing from their past, and discovering who they are now and their place in this world.

This collection of poems is for all the little girls and boys who have grown up now that ever felt alone at a time in life. You are not alone. I hope reading these poems brings you comfort, peace, and helps you feel connected to me. Through me sharing my voice through my artwork based on my lived experience I hope you can see our commonalities.

We are all just people on this large globe with no manual on how to live life "correctly" so each of us is truly doing the best we know how. Remember to be kind to yourself as you give others grace. See the humanity that lives within you and also in them. I hope you enjoy me sharing with you all a little bit of who I am.

Acknowledgments

I'd like to acknowledge all those who have ever helped and supported me throughout my life. I am grateful for everything that has been done for me and even appreciate the people and things that have inflicted pain because from it, great art and life lessons came. Thank you to all of those who are in my life currently, supporting and rooting for me.

Contents

Preface

This is a collection of poems that I wrote all during my 27th year of life in this world, with the exception of one being written at age 26 years old. 27 years of life is significant to me and my family, so I found this age to be a perfect time to work on another book. The poetry in this book represents things I have experienced in my life and how I've come to terms with them. Some of the poems included also speak about issues that are important to me and causes on fighting for. I hope my poetry helps give perspective of my view of the world but also sparks dialogue and conversation. I discuss things we don't always talk about as a nation and even within our families. I'm using my voice to express myself but never with any intent to hurt anyone else around me. I'm using my voice to express myself but never with any intent to hurt anyone else around me, just want to share parts of my story. Peace and love. I hope that you enjoy the read.

Red & Blue Flashing Lights

Can't even think about what it means to love me
as the fear of the police confines my mind
red and blue flashing lights,
heart rate increases
unconsciously going into hyperarousal every time
turn down the music as the corners of my mouth drop
as that smile fades away
because what was once funny must be put on pause
because for a moment our lives could be at stake
meanwhile, I'm sure the cop driving is carefree
wondering what's gonna be the next meal on his plate
not concerned with whether or not he's gonna eat again
because he'll be the one pointing the gun
watching the next negro bleed out yet again
at the mercy of the men in blue
"Protect and serve America & its citizens?"
then I must ask..
who are we to you?
3/5ths of a person right?
"property" to be stolen from our lands for years on end
then condemned for simply existing and living
in a country we were brought to against our will
that my ancestors not only built, from the ground up
all while being mistreated, tortured, taunted, slaughtered, killed
stripped of our culture

dismantled

systematically infiltrated when our only goal

was self love and defense

very intentionally destroyed our family units and communities

consciously keeping us divided

because there is strength in numbers

UNITY

if only we could all see our power and beauty

and join together like it's our duty

realize that we have more in common

than the instinctual fear that creeps up

every time a police car gets near

Red & Blue Flashing Lights

Tears in My Eyes

Tears in my eyes
Pain in my heart
Screams I can't cry
For you'll only label me that angry black woman
But you're murdering my people and you wonder why
Wouldn't you be angry too
Living in a world where the justice system is corrupt
Who am I supposed to turn to?
Who are we supposed to turn to?
Still fighting for our civil rights
While questioning the "sustainability" of the 14th amendment
Breaks my heart to know that one day
when I birth little black babies into this world,
I'll have to let them know that
it has never been created with us in mind
And to keep your hands where you can see them
when you get pulled over at all times
That they can't play with toy guns like other kids or
wear the hoods of their jackets on their heads
Even if it's just to go to the corner store and buy some skittles,
Be sure to let Mommy know because it could be the last time I get to hug,
kiss & tell you I love you so
"Equal protection under the law"
But you don't see us as people deserving to be here at all
Why must each of us bleed out before you start to realize that

We are people
Human beings too!
With a right to live
Whose culture you love to appropriate
Excuse me, did you say appreciate
But how can you appreciate something
that comes from a race of people
You don't even view worthy of life itself
You want our men, our music, our soul food,
our features, our curves and curls,
But has it ever occurred to you that you can steal all those things and
Still never truly know what it's like to walk in the skin I live in
Because baby black is undeniably beautiful
But it's also heavy
The weight we all carry simply for existing and the color of our skin
To fear that any wrong turn your life may end
And what is "wrong"?
Calling 911 for help when you fear there's an intruder
Only for the police to arrive and
not protect you but instead become your shooter
Then mock and disrespect you after taking your life way sooner
Than it should have ended
Leaving a family behind
Motherless, daughterless, hearts forever unmended
Because you can never replace a life
that was taken at the mercy of an entitled race
Time and time again, not only America
but the world has shown us that they don't care about my people,
Black people

And before you go saying no, that's not true
"I have friends that look just like you"
Having black friends doesn't undo
The responsibility you hold to treat each us,
not just your chosen few
As your equal and with dignity and respect
Because don't get me started,
we're actually the first and best to ever grace this earth with our existence
So remember that the next time you bump Kendrick
They not like us
It's true
No one can imitate or recreate black
We embody it in everything we do
Black is beautiful
Black is me
Black is you
Everything started with black and emerged from our culture
After we've been taken for over 400 years from our land by vultures,
But then questioned why we always bring up the topic of racism and
injustice
Like we asked for this way of life
When it's been forced upon us
You can never understand the life a black woman or man leads
So all I ask is that you put some respect on not only me, and my people,
but also where we all derived from
Love us the way you love our culture
And remember where you come from

Wish for Clarity

11:11

wish for clarity

when you said you love me,

did you mean it with sincerity

or did you mean it temporarily

until the initial spark of me & you died out

because 3 months later we're sitting in a car for hours

trying to piece together our feelings towards each other warily

feels like we've spent so much time

but trying to understand each other

is like mimes tryna read each other's minds

we know aspects of each other

but well enough to promise forever?

cause one minute I have no doubts

then the next you make me wanna shout

I love you, I do but am I too much

to ask someone to be committed to

is my idea of love and ideal partner

simply skewed to something that's not even real,

attainable true?

limiting beliefs holding me back from me and you

more inner work and growth I've gotta do

because if I'm not 100% happy with myself,

how can I be happy with you?

You Almost Fooled Me, Royalty

Anger
an emotion that I'm not used to feeling or
familiar with expressing
but your behavior and actions
and then the replay of them in my head
has triggered this feeling
of boiling rage inside of me
causing my calm nature and
mild mannered temperament into question
when I asked you not to lie to me,
did you take it as a suggestion?
but I'm confused because you
promised me that you'd always be honest
hold my heart dear
told you it was my most prized possession,
only to find out you were nothing but a con artist
the way you tricked me by
persuading me to believe that your love was true
Simply through narcissistic techniques of love bombing,
which to me was something new
flattered by the gifts, kind gestures, and words
thought it was cute how you wanted
to spend every waking moment with me
not knowing that it was all part of your strategy
it was like a game, sport for you to get me

to fall in love with the person you pretended to be
and I applaud you
shit
you deserve an award
because I truly thought you adored me
and that I meant something to you
only to find out that it was all fabricated
and everything but sincere and true
I never thought you would hurt me and play in my face,
not only once, but multiple times, you chose to
guess you easily get bored and
constantly need to entertain someone new
I just thought with how much time we were spending and talking
that you couldn't possibly have time for anyone else
but I guess I was mistaken about that too
while you fed me fantasies and fairytale
dreams that you never intended to fulfill
of marriage, and children, a big happy house on the hill
we hadn't decided on countryside or city life but
you promised me you'd follow me to the end of the earth
and like a fool I believed it
but I thank the universe for revealing to me the true you
someone who I would never
ever want to be eternally committed to
whew
that was a close call
I could've lost it all
and by that, I mean me
my sanity, my strength, my pure heart

the woman I've grown to be and at the core always was
but now from this pain,
I can become a better 3.0 version of me
someone who will recognize
when it's not love, even when it claims to be
to use my discernment and
rid myself of all the insincere
and negative energy around me,
trying to dim my light,
take advantage of my heart, or put me down
because in case you forgot
I am a queen, and I refuse to let anyone remove my crown

Played the Lotto, Won ME

You asked me why I hate gambling?
it's cause I did the shit everyday for 18 years straight
coming home to an environment that was always unpredictable
roll the dice
blow on em this time, roll again
bet you I'm walking into a hostile environment 9 times out of 10
will it be nice Mommy today
or one who's upset that you did something imperfectly because my best
will never be enough
clean that up faster
and when I talk to you, you better look at me in the eyes and answer
I slowly learned the "right" things to say to try to keep the storm at bay
there was no preventing the outbursts and chaos completely
because looking back hindsight, they barely had anything to do with me
but shit I'd like to take a moment to applaud myself
because girl you mastered walking on eggshells and thinking three steps
ahead of the next because it was not safe to act without thinking
but to triple think may just possibly prevent a beating
or stern talking to that lasted till the sun came up or
until she was blue in the face
until all the anger and rage dissipate
"if you can't handle me, you can't handle the real world"
had me terrified of what was to come

once I grew up and faced it on my own

but to my surprise it wasn't nearly as mentally taxing,

psychologically draining, and scary

as what I had experienced my whole life

seeing now that the things I was indirectly taught and learned

don't apply to everyday life

that I can actually have my own voice and opinions too

say what I want to and do what I want to do

in any way I want to

how fast or slow

there's no punishment for being authentically me and choosing to show

up however I please?

but who is me?

underneath all of the programming and people pleasing

forget assuming how others want you to behave and acting accordingly

trying to fit into every place you go looking for acceptance

because you never got it from your parents

so I have a message as a grown woman to the younger me, Baby Ashaki

I love you so much and have always done my best to keep you safe

know that things always get better and now we are free

hold my hand, there's something I want you to see.

8 Ball

My white therapist thought I was a drug addict
sorry not addict, just occasional user
now that it may seem like she thought that because I'm black
and well like most white people, stereotypes could've consumed her
but no ya girl has had a past where I've gone a little crazy
bouncing off the walls, figuratively that is
but even though I may have been manic,
I know for a fact I never said I did an 8 ball
or was an addict
I shared the story of encountering people behind bars who spoke of
what I thought was a childhood toy
that you shake a little to the left and right
for a yes, no, or maybe after asking a question about a boy
Nope, she in fact meant cocaine
and till this day I couldn't bring myself to try it
but by the way her eyes lit up talking about it
I could see that it was her way of self medicating to ease her pain
despite the fact that when she's sober all the pain remains
I use to try to escape the weight of my sorrows through kissing the sky
every night routinely get high
it was like I needed that shit to get by
because the pain had become unbearable and emotions too big to feel
no one knew that I was only a few pills away from ending it all
poof, vanish, dissipate, fade away
the death of me
what I thought would be a happy day

Is Your Cup Full Enough In a Room Full of Cups

My whole life has been
SORRY am I too much of an inconvenience?
Am I taking up too much air breathing?
Too much space?
Being?
Don't say what
Say pardon me
And when you find yourself bored
Sing it out in a song spelling bee
Never knew that acquiring knowledge
Growing intellectually
Would only make you proud of me
If I receive degree after degree because
One is not enough
And my success is truly an attempt at making you feel good enough
Sorry that may have sounded disrespectful
I may be hurt and only view life from my own lense
Not sure of what another's life has been outside of my own
even my family's
I just know that sometimes I feel alone
And the success I've been chasing
that's so heavily tied to my academic worth is taking a toll
Had a hard time at one point separating me
from my value if I got less than A
Until life became so overwhelming and unbearable

That I didn't have the capacity to go to class each day
So got a semester of F's at a university most dream of attending
While my dreams consisted of all the years of pain I experienced ending
I'm not saying it's a crime to want the youth in your family
to make you proud and be an example of black excellence,
because we have endured a lot as a race
And the world has placed
So many odds against us
I'm just saying this journey hasn't been easy
To have to work 10x harder than my peers
So please give me grace and hug when you see me
Cause yes, I'm that strong black woman I watched
the woman in my family embody
But every once in a while, we all need love from somebody

Dance With the Wind

Just when you thought it'd be a breeze
and life may momentarily be at ease
the next problem arises
just one of a different kind
I don't know what it is about my nature that makes me so naive
to think that life can be nothing but rainbows, sunshine, and pure joy
probably the optimist in me
and my never give up spirit that I attribute to my Buddhist philosophy
got God looking down on me while I'm crying like
girl please
hold on a little longer because everything happening
right now is a part of the plan
present not to be the end of me but rebirth
moment to build me into everything I'm meant to be
for far too long failed to recognize the greatness in me
the beauty in me and that I am truly worthy
of all the good things in life,
abundance of love, laughter, success, joy and so much more
but what I'm going through currently is necessary to teach me a lesson
to carry me through life
so I can shine much brighter than ever before
universe testing me to see if I'm truly committed to the version of me
that's living the life I've always longed for since I was a child

alignment matched with preparation
and tools to cope and navigate any situation
trust that synchronicities will occur
making sense of all the chaos currently flooding my shore
for I know it's only temporary
URGENT MESSAGE to you
don't lose yourself even when times get heavy
hang in there, you will smile and feel a true joy again
when life gets a lil more steady
in the meantime dance with the wind

Mirror

Wow the more I see you clearly for who you are
and not what I want you to be or
who I know you'd tried to be after me
bringing up my needs or concerns so effortlessly
I think we share the trait in common of adaptability
and learning how to act how we think those around us want us to
so confused don't know the true you
Though I used to think your effort to change and lack of anger
when I brought up something that
bothered me or a need I had that wasn't being met
was top tier and made this all worth working through
problem is I just don't believe it's sincere
and the more I spend time with you,
the more I realize I am not the one for you
nor you for me
I may require too much of you by analyzing situations
then asking you deep questions reflecting on not only your behavior
but what that action was tied to
was it the lack of feeling love from a parent growing up?
growing up being emotionally abandoned? abused?
or was it never feeling good enough that makes you seek
validation in how many women you can pull
not believing you're deserving of true love
so when I say I'm all in, you pull away
not with your words but your selfsabotaging actions

betray me and erase all trust that I may have had in you at all
but to be clear, I'm not claiming to be a saint
or woman fully healed from all her trauma
I have imperfections too
but I've for many years been aware of them seeking help and healing
through therapy, frequencies, nature,
movement, mindfulness, breathing too
I thought I knew you but
you met a version of me that is now dead
because I've rebirthed a new
I'm grateful for the time you've served in my life
but I know there will come a time for someone new
For me
and you
I loved you, but I don't think we're meant to be
Twin flames
your presence in my life sparked something new
and the pain you caused led to my personal growth
so while I once cried tears over you
and your actions left me hating men,
not sure when I'll be able to trust one again
I still thank you
because after you, I found true love
in the place I should've been looking all along
Inside of me
Internally happy

Inherent Greatness

Baby girl, NEVER
And I mean, NEVER forget who tf you are
Baby you radiate, shine, glow
Midas? Ain't got shit on you
Everything you touch turns to gold
Simply because the soil in which you come from is rich, fertile
Didn't know your roots went so deep
& that despite the many attempts to destroy them
And make the plant to grow from it become weak, never bear fruit,
die off and no longer exist
They underestimated your strength
Essence
Resilience

Foolish

Silly Me
so foolish to think you had changed
in such a short amount of time too
that dog mentality
fuck bitches, get money shit is ingrained within you
would never be your only one
and not because I'm less of a woman
or not enough
but because you haven't came to terms with your own demons
who you truly are
so you project onto me and try to suppress your feeling of inadequacy
with validation from as many women you can get to fall
for who you pretend to be in the beginning
meanwhile you don't know who you truly are
people can only meet you as deeply as they've met themselves
and you a stranger to your inner self
but I see you
behind all the facade and artificial charm
I pray you fall in love with who you see in the mirror
before you try to get another girl on your arm

Ocean Temperature Rising

Man since when did summer in the Bay Area
get up to and in some parts over 103
and only 97 degrees in the East Coast Washington, DC
where it's humid and muggy
but was as cold as 22 degrees at the beginning of 2023
and past years SF only got 15 inches of rain in all 365 days of 2022
the seasons are CHANGING
what is our word coming to
but it's not just the weather, our water blues
what's the fate of our oceans if we don't do something soon
because climate change is causing the temperature
of our oceans to increase,
due to the neglectful eye & careless actions of humanity
things that humans do like burning fossil fuels is increasing levels
of carbon dioxide & other greenhouse gases in the atmosphere
while most of us don't even have the decency to discuss
what's happening on our social media platforms or even with our peers
like ways to adapt to this issue by maybe limiting greenhouse emissions
or even creating an End Climate Change & Save Our Oceans Petition
we need more people on a mission
to help prevent the massive and irreversible impact
of growing temperatures on ocean ecosystems
many species & marine vertebrates,
from eels and turtles to reef building coral & fish
depend on ocean currents for reproduction & nutrients
warmer waters cause coral bleaching, impacting the coral reef ecosystems

that are home to an array of marine biodiversity,
and this not only affects sea life you see
they provide crucial sources of food for people like you and me
despite the fact that 3 billion people rely on fish
as a leading source of proteins
& warmer waters affect the development and growth of most fish
I know most of you won't listen until I tell you this
warmer ocean waters threaten food security and supply
imagine not being able to crack open that crab leg for a fat piece of meat
or pescatarians going extinct simply because there's not enough to eat
rising ocean temperatures also increase the prevalence of disease
whether it be through direct transmission
from consuming these marine species
or from infections of wounds
and diseases exposed to marine environments
and don't get me started on sea levels rising as glaciers melt
having the potential to flood cities we know and love
killing and displacing people like you and me
bye bye Mami and Nola baby
which together hold a population of about 817,000 people
brought to their death or displaced
now wouldn't that be crazy,
not just the U.S
cities would flood all over the world
so let's not wait until they're underwater,
food is scarce & diseases are thriving
Promise you'll do something to
HELP OUR OCEANS
before temperature rates keep rising

It's Ok

It's ok to accept love?
It's ok to accept love
It's ok to allow someone to love me?
It's ok to allow someone to love you
It's ok ask for help?
It's ok to ask for and receive help
At this big age of 27 shocked to find out that
all the love you give to others
Doesn't have to be one sided even though you never viewed it as
transactional or minded
But honey love can be reciprocal, in fact it should be
It's ok to allow someone to do something
for you when they offer and want to
Baby girl, let people show you that they love you

#1 Top Viewer

Checking my page daily
would've thought you had enough of me
but I guess that feeling's never satiated,
though you never reach out to text or call
but you do be checking in on me
seeing what I'm doing,
how I'm living
what I'm posting
viewing from a far
just watching but never showing
LOVE
At this point you might as well be paying me
for a subscription to access into my life
because it must be a form of entertainment
for you to watch but not reach out
when you actually know me in real life
but my bad it's just a post, social media
fun & games right
façades and carefully constructed versions of us portrayed
I just never thought of you to be fake
say you have love for me
but do me in the worst ways
cause when was the last time you called and checked on me to say
how are you doing?
I love you and if you ever need me, I'm here
Everything is gonna be okay

Black Man, You Are Enough Just as You Are

A man consumed with obligations of the busy world around him
married not to another person, but the stress that refuses to leave his side
worry and the weight of the world that keeps him up at night
or could it be the sirens, flashing lights, or cries and words spoken from
the unlucky ones down on their luck
with no home for a door to even crack open
but if enough change was thrown their way, maybe they'd have enough
for a bottle at the end of the day
seal, unbroken
but that only contributes to the sleepless nights and mental demons
one has to fight while the moon is in the sky
see, a drunk man is much louder than a sober one
but regardless of how loud, society refuses to hear a man's cries
said he's leaving the city, and you've got people questioning why
have you tried asking him what he feels inside?
because he told me that despite having air in his lungs, he feels dead
and he can't escape the negative thoughts in his head
feels like if he can't make money to have a means to provide
then women will toss him to the side
and find a man who will pay for all the things
eventually even a diamond ring,
the woman, not knowing that she's merely an investment on his future
through her love and life that he intends to procreate
he believes that society will finally celebrate
his existence and honor him as a man

because he was never taught or told
that he was enough and innately worthy, but
black man I see you
He responded, "I am enough just as I am?"

Christmas Eve

It's like a younger sibling of 3
who already may suspect that Santa
isn't real from the lack of enthusiasm
he can see his older brother and sister feel
and words spoken of peers at school that he overhears
but still manages to try his hardest to stay awake on Christmas Eve
after putting cookies and milk out for Mr. Claus by the tree
but somehow minutes turn to hours and his eyes get heavier and heavier
as the excitement can't hold him any longer
so reluctantly, he falls asleep
I find myself just like that boy, filled with hope
of the possibility that maybe this time you can be good to me
after shattering my fragile heart
I have speculations & gut feelings that it may not be as sincere and true as
you're telling me
can a liar stop the instinct or urge to deceive?
how about if I ask 3 more times over again,
then add at the end a pretty please
because all I ever did was love you for who you truly are
or at least which you allowed me to see
not knowing the secrets kept behind the scenes
performance
lights, camera, action
The role you played was convincing and believable in many ways
so excuse me for getting swept off my feet

when I should've been eating popcorn from the theater seat
merely entertained by what I saw before me
but instead I was deeply enthralled
and charmed by the lines that were far way too corny
as I told you, words of affirmation was one of the main ways to my heart
then I'm sure you pieced together by the depth
in which I communicate and talk
that a little mental stimulation just might get past the 3rd base mark
but is that all you ever wanted for me from the start
and then made it your mission to convince me
that you were also also hopeless romantic at heart
or do you really crave a love that's true?
one that won't leave you hurt and feeling blue?
help you to become the purest version of you?
A love so abundant that it shines light
on the darkest parts of your soul
and instead of judging, holds its arms open wide
to embrace all of you fully,
a whole
person
I am a person
a living being that you said you loved
the same way you say you love the sun,
but you chase the shade to stay hidden from its rays
and also the same way you claim to love the rain, but you stay inside to
keep dry on rainy days
So I wonder, what does love truly mean to you?
and are you capable of it?
giving it, not just receiving?

leaving me like that little boy on Christmas Eve, hoping
still believing
that you are real
all I know is that if I do give you another chance
you better not fuck it up
Deal?

A Special Day That I've Never Got to Celebrate

Funny how dates pass
reminding you of the loved one you once had
in your life,
to some degree, right?
remembering that today is your birthday
wanting to send you well wishes
give you your flowers, bouquet
but I know that you'll refuse to meet me halfway
& even just respond to a message I say
you stay doing me in the worst ways
but it doesn't subtract the abundance of love my heart has for you
as all I wanted was a sisterly love growing up
something I never knew
to be honest, it hurts that you have no interest
or wanna get to know me too
for years I have prayed that you'd come around
thought maybe once you have kids,
you'll want them to know their Auntie
who would spoil them rotten and give them all of the love
you must have forgotten
that I have for you
simply because you are my big sister
and I share blood with you

Think Critically

Speechless
bear with me as I try to find the words to say
um
hmm
where do I begin?
should I start with my initial thoughts?
or the ones that just came pouring in?
it's like for so long I've thought before I reacted
that it almost feels like to take action
without thinking beforehand is a sin
but if I don't say truly what's on my mind and
have my thoughts, beliefs, and behaviors aligned
can true authenticity ever win?
People say be yourself, but they really need to stay within certain
parameters that box you in
to not deviate so far from societal norms
to maintain the narrative that we must conform
because change is scary to some,
people love to push away and tend to make fun
of things they don't understand or have previous exposure to
so why do I have to suffer over your fear of something new?
ignorance is something we're all subjected to
but the more you know, the better you feel called to do
So wake up
open your eyes

look around
question everything you have been taught
take note of who told you that,
the source,
the way in which it was delivered to you and others,
at a grand or small scale?
and who benefits from the information being spread?
what's their intent?
just be a critical thinker
use your head

27 In Your Shoes

27

So if I was in your shoes right now,
I'd have a 10 year old child?
The thought of that to me is wild
I'm just barely learning how to fully take care of myself
Another mouth to feed?
Big brown eyes looking up to me,
Depending on me for everything?
I can't fathom the sacrifices you must have had to make for me
And I know it couldn't have been easy
Not the way media tries to portray teen moms on VH1 TV
Nothing to be glamorized
But I do want to applaud the way you always made it look so easy
The epitome of strong & resilient
Chose to have me despite what others were feeling
Looking out for your future and the life you had ahead
But you saw me in yours
And for that, I'm forever grateful
For everything you did
You always provided and made a way for us,
even when I'm sure you didn't know how
Looking back, you turned a little something into a lot
There wasn't much I wanted as I child that I never got
From the Bratz dolls to the Wii and even fresh new Pastry shoes
Our family wasn't perfect

But you dedicated your life to do the best to raise me

Every year made my birthday so special

A little reality hit when I grew up and found out

it's not in fact a national holiday

I'm joking, but the way in which you've celebrated me

Has NEVER gone unnoticed or taken for granted

I appreciate it in the deepest way

You have such a big heart

And show love to people in the grandest of ways

That's probably something I got from you

I didn't realize until today

I guess what I'm tryna say

Is… thank you Mom

For all the sacrifices you made for me,

Some I know I will never understand until I have children myself

Thank you for carrying me for 9 months and bringing me into this world

Without you, I wouldn't be here

Looking at you is like looking in a mirror twin

I'm glad to know that with age, my beauty will never fade

I guess I'm just tryna say

I love you in a million different ways

Green Tea

Steam coming out the teapot
it's getting a lil hot
provoking, triggering, prying, poking the bear
then act surprised when it stands on its two legs and lets out a growl
louder than you anticipated and now you're scared
but the bear just wanted peace and for you to leave it be
so he's not concerned with hurting you
he's just trying to figure what next he's going to eat
because no one goes to the forests and feeds the wildlife
they're not pets, they roam free
and with freedom comes full responsibility for taking care of oneself, Me
scared of what the future will bring, but I just know it'll be great
because boiling water on a stove is often times used
to make a hot cup of nutritious green tea
I don't know about you
but that brings some sort of peace to me

Creative Baby

Well I'm a creative baby
it's kinda embedded in me
comes naturally
I turn misery & pain into art
show
got my feelings on display
come look at my inner being
through my writings
and greet the demons that haunt me
but my positive energy and
innate light keep them at bay
because my heart is genuine and pure
but I'm human shit, what can I say
never been perfect
despite many attempts to be
only was tryna live up
to what was expected of me
not knowing that I was born great already
and actually worthy
of all the love I so easily give those around me
waiting for someone to tell me
take a seat please
cause while you were nurturing others,
I noticed your leaves are wilting
and hanging low

You water everybody else
but baby don't forget
you also need water to grow
The healer needs healing
The planner needs surprises
The giver also needs to receive
The thoughtful needs to be thought of
The considerate needs to be considered
I know you're heart is big and
you don't mind being a giver
but I just want you to consider
who you allow in your circle
because baby you naturally
elevate those around you
not only go to bat for the ones
you love and care about
but consider them in everything you do
Baby girl you bring a lot to the plate
so after you cook the dinner
Let someone else set the table
Enjoy good company
Because baby girl with this one you ate

27 Years of Life

27 years old
A life that has been full of events
so many stories untold
and some I'm still trying to learn the lesson from
and find meaning of why things occurred
but I know that without everything I've experienced
I would not be the very person I am today, standing in front of you
who can genuinely smile and recognize
who she sees while looking in the mirror
because I have worked on loving who I am
and building a true connection, relationship with myself
because I'm the only one who will be with me through everything
thankful for all the experiences in life
I've been fortunate enough to have, the good and even the bad
tears, pain, trauma, heartbreak, difficulties,
setbacks and all that has tried to keep me down
because through overcoming all of that, my joy and hopefulness remains
to know that my ancestors were once in chains and that I live a life
that they could only ever imagine in their wildest dreams
and though we still face discrimination currently,
things are not what they once were
so remember that the next time you feel life is hard
there were generations of our people who endured slavery and injustice,
inhumane practices and constant murdering,
lynching, slaughtering of my people

So recognize that in 2024 we have a little more rights & freedom
I encourage you all to soar and fly like eagles
use your voice
it's ok to be heard and to speak
stand up for injustice when you see it
to not do so would be weak
because don't you believe all humans are deserving of having rights
and being treated as equals
27 years of life for me is how much time some people spend behind bars
kept away from the world, not able to see its beauty and live free,
peacefully amongst society
so I guess I'm trying to remind you to care about not only your own life
but also of those around you
fight for causes that you find important
we should all be tryna do better and take care of this planet
that we share with each other and all call home

About the Author

Ashaki Satomi Scott is a 28 year old Bay Area Native from California. She is a recent graduate of Cal State East Bay and is working in her community as a social worker now. She has always been concerned with the welfare and well being of others, so she feels honored to be doing the work she does. She has been writing poetry her whole life since elementary school, and despite taking a break from creative writing for a few years, never lost her way with words. She is actively writing again now and can't invision life without it.

This is her second published book. Her first novel, "The Average Girl, Me" was published in March 2024 and is composed of poetry she wrote throughout her whole life. This book specifically focuses on poetry she has written more recently and the majority of the poems in this novel were written during her 27th year of life. The poems in this book displays some of her range of ability to incorporate different styles of poetry amongst various topics. The poems in this book are very unfiltered, raw, uncut, and some might say blunt. I hope you can appreciate her vulnerability and courage to be authentic in a world filled with people who don't know what it means to be real. Keep an open mind while reading her poetry and braise yourself for how her words may make you feel.